Deep gratitude to my friends and family for all of your support and guidance throughout the creation of this book.

Until We Meet Again is dedicated with love and gratitude to my parents, Judy and Bo Porchuk, and all of the animal companions we have loved and cared for throughout our lives. Growing up on a farm was a gift.

UNTIL WE MEET AGAIN

written by:
Melissa Lyons

Illustrated by:
Patricia Henderson

There is a place in my heart where you will always be
and it's full of memories of just you and me.

Wet kisses and snuggles, my nose on your face,
we've shared many moments we'll always embrace.

This part of our journey has come to an end,
so here are some words to help your heart mend.

Take time to read them, I ask this of you.
I hope when you're finished, you won't feel so blue.

Please find a safe space that will allow you to feel.
Open your heart and let yourself heal.

Close your eyes for a moment and take time to breathe.
I can live in your heart, if you choose to believe.

I want you to know that it's OK to cry.
Take the time that you need and look to the sky.

Let me go with your love, please set me free.
Things will get better. Trust and you'll see.

Look for rainbows and butterflies and clues that I'll send.
They will be your reminders that our bond will not end.

You will see things and feel things that remind you of me.
Finding joy in the memories is your master key.

We learned lots together,
both finding our way.
Our adventures were fun.
We made the most of each day.

There were days you came home, not feeling quite right.
As soon as you saw me, your heart filled with light.

Throughout my life you taught me tricks and much more.
Now it's my turn to nudge you to soar.

There is some advice that I would like to impart.
Can you let me do this? Will you open your heart?

When we were together, you put your troubles on hold.
I gave you the courage to let life unfold.

I taught you things as you watched me live,
unconditional love and to always forgive.

Believe it or not, you have all that you need.

You're an amazing person and you will succeed.

Trust that your love can release all your fears.
This lesson alone can guide you for years.

You can't change the past, this you should know.
You can change the future and where you will go.

In every moment you have choices to make.
Your path is determined by the roads that you take.

Allow your mind time to unwind and be free.

Be as kind to yourself as you were to me.

Please live for today, fill your life full of love.
Imagine me with you, inside and above.

Look for hope, love and joy in all that you do.
Imagine your life with your dreams coming true.

And...
Until we meet again,
remember...

Melissa Lyons is an award-winning author, coach & speaker who empowers people to become the person they were meant to be. She focuses on Hope, Love and Gratitude.

LEARN MORE:

www.Melissa-Lyons.com

Also by Melissa Lyons:

I Will Always Love You
A Journey From Grief and Loss to Hope and Love

I Will Always Love You is a simple, thought provoking and deeply moving story that takes minutes to read and can last a lifetime in your heart. The intention of this book is to bring peace and comfort to those who have lost a loved one or experienced some type of personal loss. It offers hope and a sense of knowing that our loved ones could be somewhere happy and free. It reminds us that our deliberate choices can alter the way we respond to loss and can have the power to bring us a sense of joy and the transcendence that lifts us to a higher place of living. Perfect for children and adults, this unique book is unlike anything available on the market.

ISBN 978-0-9959491-0-2

Additional Resources

If you feel pain in your heart and it sometimes hurts to breathe, you are not alone. When it feels like you are walking with a bullet in your heart, please know that there is help. It can come in the form of a phone call, a Skype chat or a face to face visit with someone who can relate to your pain. There are tools that can give you respite to your anguish and a supportive pathway to your healing. For additional resources visit our website.

www.Melissa-Lyons.com/Resources